PLAIN TALK

Richard Rollins

Photocomposition by
Société Arts Graphiques Composition Paris

Published by Paris Press San Francisco

Printed in the United States of America
Thanks to my friend piero toaldo for his help with this book

ISBN: 978-1-7371412-0-4

PLAIN TALK

JEAN DRYER: PASO ROBLES, TEXAS, AUGUST 11

"Nobody thought well of me. You can say I felt sorry for myself but that's not the whole truth. There were other circumstances. Circumstances beyond my control."

ABE LUFUS: CORDERO MINE, NEV.,
AUGUST 15

"It's fifteen miles from here to the interstate. Before
airplanes there was nothing out here as far as the eye could
see. I've been a sorry assed son of a bitch all my life but
I never killed a man and I never refused a helping hand to
anyone who needed it."

DORTHY (DOT) PARKER: LANGTREE TRAILER PARK, YUMA, ARIZ., AUGUST 15

"What's gone is gone. Sometimes I'm glad. You can't kill a chicken without there isn't blood. I've wished away half my life. I'm not proud of that but I'm not ashamed."

ELVA JENNINGS: SWEETWATER COUNTY, WYO., AUGUST 15

"It's a very sad thing to be not right in your mind. It's hard most all the time. It's the very, very saddest when you know."

SHERILEE GRANGER: CARSON CITY, NEV., AUGUST 15

"They want to think he talked me into it. Let 'em. It
isn't so. It was me. I was the one. He was older and he
wasn't strong but he treated me kind."

MARY T.: RODEO GROUNDS, CHEYENNE, WYO., AUGUST 16

"'Be happy and laugh.' My Momma said that. 'You can be pretty, Mary T.,' she'd say. 'You can be pretty as any of 'em.' But it isn't so."

CISSY: JACKPOT, NEV., AUGUST 16

"I asked him to marry me. I wanted to be married.
Now I know. It's not for me."

HOUGHTON CLEARY: DEL RIO, TEXAS, AUGUST 16

"I once beat a man. Beat him bad. For no reason. I can't do that anymore. I just can't."

SUE ANN DYERSON: POCATELLO, IDAHO, AUGUST 19

"Sue Ann sounds pretty. It's a made up name. I made it up. You don't have to keep the name you were born with. You don't. There's nothing says so."

IDA MAY BECKER: SALT LAKE CITY, UTAH, AUGUST 19

"I've never told anyone and I never will. They pestered
me with it so over the years I just stopped talking.
Sometimes I get afraid I won't be strong enough. 'Mother,'
they say or 'Grandma, please!' But I won't talk."

CHESTER REDMAN: LOGGING CAMP, MEDICINE BOW NATIONAL FOREST, WYO., AUGUST 19

"The Brotherhood lives right up here in the mountains. Up in caves in the highest peaks. Every day they turn a page in your book of life. When they turn the page that calls you, you got to go."

MRS. ELMORE W. HARRIS: BAKERSFIELD, CALIF., AUGUST 20

"I'd had enough of winter and scratching. The kids were raised but he didn't want to. I said it's go now or I'm gone. Six months later he was dead. Now I'm married again."

CHARLEEN BLACK JR.: 4-WAY CAFE, WELLS, NEV., AUGUST 20

"I didn't want the baby. I never did. Now I'm glad.
I don't mind what she does. Even when she spits up."

BILLY BLACK JR.: 4-WAY CAFE, WELLS, NEV., AUGUST 20

"She fell outta bed this morning. My wife was supposed
to be watching her. She fell outta bed yesterday. I
said, 'Don't be doing that to my daughter.' I told her
I was gonna have to talk to her real serious. She knows
what I mean."

CHARLIE (RED) THOMPSON: ROCK SPRINGS, WYO., AUGUST 22

"It happened right here. Right on the porch steps. I'd lost my job over to the mine. I was drinking again. Didn't have no money. Didn't have nothing. Everything I'd ever had was gone. I went down on my knees. Right here on the porch steps. That's when it happened."

DELROE JESSUP: HUNTSVILLE, TEXAS, AUGUST 26

"Kids ain't dogs. Be a whole hell of a lot better this
way on his mother. You can say the bad fall farthest from
the tree but a sin is a sin and ain't no amount of money
going to put it right."

LAUREL RUSSEL: BAGGS, WYO., AUGUST 27

"Had one in the lambing pens last spring. A little black critter with two heads. Tom cut their throats."

DIANE (DEE DEE) HUNTINGTON: TULSA, OKLA., AUGUST 28

"The first baby came right after the marriage. We had two
more while David was at the university. My mother said,
'You picked him, you stick to him.' Then we had this last
one, a boy."

BUDDY DOBBS JR.: BARSTOW, CALIF., AUGUST 28

"I know I frighten people but I don't mean to. It's
'cause I'm big. But I don't feel big I feel small. Sometimes
I get afraid and I forget."

JENNIFER BOWLS: LOS ANGLES, CALIF., AUGUST 28

"Of course that's nothing to be proud of, leaving your husband and leaving your child, but it doesn't mean you're not a good mother."

REV. BILLY (PAT) ARMSTRONG: COEUR D'ALENE, IDAHO, AUGUST 29

"I spoke with the Lord and He told me to build a ministry
outside El Paso. It was fertile ground for the Lord's work
and I had a new house and fine clothes and a Cadillac car.
Then my wife stabbed me and I had to leave town."

SHIRLY JEAN WHITELY: HILLSBOROUGH, CALIF., AUGUST 30

"The most important thing is to be happy, to wake up happy everyday and to be happy all day long."

ABNER STRICKLIN: VERNAL, UTAH, AUGUST 30

''Take these here sticks. One short and one long. Don't mean a damn thing. Hold 'em like so in your fist they make a cross.''

VERNON T. JAMES: TWENTYNINE PALMS, CALIF., AUGUST 30

"There shouldn't be no sex outside marriage. It's unlawful. That's a fact."

SILAS GREEN: KEMMERER, LINCOLN COUNTY, WYO., SEPTEMBER 1

"Here abouts is all high plains. Sagebrush, sand,
greasewood. Don't look like much but I like it. It's
hard country. It's dry in summer and freezing cold in
winter. You have to get in the dry washes, the canyons.
There's eagle in there, antelope, coyote, jackrabbit. I
seen mountain lion tracks one time. There's fossil fish
from millions of years ago when this was all water. There's
hunting caves. I found arrowheads and pottery plenty. I
found this cache of corn once. I seen this cave high up
on a canyon wall. Didn't look like there was no way a
man could get up there but I found some hand holds
chipped in the wall. The kernals was all gone but the
husks was there hard as rock."

DAVID STANDING: WIND RIVER, WYO., SEPTEMBER 2

"Sure I horse around. Sometimes I get drunk. There ain't a fucking thing to do. You feel like shit."

JANET ANN DEAN: SAN FRANCISCO, CALIF., SEPTEMBER 2

"Maybe I do want to be taken care of for the rest of my life but I don't want to be judged for it."

MABEL LOUISE DANIEL: ST. GEORGE, UTAH, SEPTEMBER 3

"I was raised to tell the truth and I raised my kids
that way. It's the kids gonna suffer. The government
lied. Lied to all of us. They didn't have to there
weren't any need."

JUNIOR DAWSON: THERMOPOLIS, WYO., SEPTEMBER 4

"I broke every major bone in my body once. Some
of 'em twice. The right leg I busted four times.
Then I quit."

MARY STOCKLER: BISMARK, NORTH DAKOTA, SEPTEMBER 4

"Sweet talk is candy. Men don't understand that. They
think nice words is nails, they gonna break their teeth
on 'em."

PATRICK THOMAS (TOMMY) CHAN: ROCK SPRINGS, WYO., SEPTEMBER 5

"Saturday nights me and my buddies drive down to the river. We build a big bonfire and sit around and drink. Sometimes we get pretty drunk and jump off the cliffs. Most times someone almost drowns."

ELSIE TAYLOR: FISHING BRIDGE CAMPGROUND, YELLOWSTONE NATIONAL PARK, WYO., SEPTEMBER 6

"We've never had a real home. We've lived our whole
married lives out of trailers and cab overs. Tents was
the worst it ever got. Frank worked bridges and dams
mostly. He helped build the Dunbarten, the Telico,
worked on the rapid train tunnel out in San Francisco.
We lived on the sides of mountains in snow, rain, you
name it. Once down in Cora we had a house when Frank
was working on the Palisades. We were only in it about
a year though and it weren't ours so it don't really
count."

FRANK TAYLOR: FISHING BRIDGE CAMPGROUND, YELLOWSTONE NATIONAL PARK, WYO., SEPTEMBER 7

''I just quit. I said to hell with it and went fishing.
They wouldn't let you do the job right no more. I've
worked dams won't last twenty years. You can talk
'til you're blue in the face. Don't mean a thing.
It's money talks. If they think you're trouble,
you're gonna get your check and be gone. Union won't
back you. I don't need it. I done my time.''

JACK RAWLY: FALLON, NEV.,
SEPTEMBER 8

"I'd run a load of bucking horses clear down to Cedar
City and I was coming home. At first I thought it was
headlights. Another truck running down a side road along
the highway. It got brighter and brighter and I could see
it weren't headlights. I was doing maybe eighty. It come right
up along side the truck. A big ball of greenish light.
Then someone called my name."

GEORGE THURGOOD: WHITEFISH, MONT., SEPTEMBER 11

"Atlanta, that's the place for clean pussy."

PENELOPE REDHOUSE: RAPID CITY, SOUTH DAKOTA, SEPTEMBER 11

"I don't want to forget. I never want to forget. I want
to remember every single thing. Everyone who was in on it.
I never want to forget who they are and what they done."

T.J.: SOUTH CITY, SAN FRANCISCO, CALIF., SEPTEMBER 12

"Wayne's in the house eating dinner. This dude pulls up on a motorcycle. Wayne's got his knife out but this dude's got a gun, Jim. Wayne lets go the knife and this dude kicks Wayne three or four times in the balls."

EDIE BUCKLER: ROCK SPRINGS, WYO., SEPTEMBER 12

"Men are shits. If they don't get killed on you, they'll
leave you for something younger. You want the imitation
for the long haul, the one has got the steady job, house
and insurance."

EUGENE CRAWLY: PROVO, UTAH, SEPTEMBER 15

"After I got out, I turned my life over to the Lord.
The Lord has been good to me. I have a fine house now
and a good job, a loving wife and three fine children."

CHARLE E. (CHUCK) HAGAR: HOUSTON, TEXAS, SEPTEMBER 16

"Sometimes I get these ugly and perverted ideas. They scare the hell out of me. I don't know how they get into my mind and I damn sure don't want to think about it."

JOHN HILL: ELKO, NEV., SEPTEMBER 17

"I won't live longer than other men. I don't expect to and I don't need to."

DOLPH BECKER: MEETEETSE, WYO., SEPTEMBER 17

"Americans are a fearful people. They were afraid of mountains lions and wolves and bears and they stamped them out. But they never stamped out the fear."

MAUREEN (BABE) HASKINS: OGDEN, UTAH, SEPTEMBER 19

"In our family there has never been one single case of mental abnormality or one single case of physical abnormality."

ALBERT (BUZZ) HASKINS: OGDEN, UTAH, SEPTEMBER 19

"There's some people that's better'n others. They just are. They're born that way. It's meant to be."

DORTHEA STEVENS: ABIQUIU, NEW MEXICO, SEPTEMBER 20

"There's times when I wish I could take things back.
What's left me is my bed to lay in. You can work hard
all your life, you can walk out over these hills for
thirty miles and come home exhausted. But it's not
enough."

JIM CODY: GREAT FALLS, MONT., SEPTEMBER 20

"I grew up believing you could count on a man but you couldn't never trust a woman. I've trusted men and been burned bad. I've mistrusted women and they proved to be true."

DARLENE MILLER-TAKAMURA: SANTA MONICA, CALIF., SEPTEMBER 21

"I have a glass of juice in the morning and sometimes I
have a cup of coffee. For lunch I have a hard boiled egg
or cheese and an apple or banana. Maybe I'll have a glass
of white wine with dinner, a small green salad and a piece
of fish. I use the exercise machine everyday and I jog
and on the weekends I swim laps at the club."

CLAUDE DUNALLY: DUBOIS, WYO., SEPTEMBER 22

"I had the roof on when the first snow come but the floor weren't finished and the windows was covered in plastic. There weren't any electricity or running water but I was fixing to get us a good wood burning stove and we had a pump out back. She left the end of December and I just quit building."

PATTY (P.J.) BROOKS: RAWLINS, WYO., SEPTEMBER 23

"Even if I am young it doesn't mean I don't know.
I don't believe what people tell me, I don't. Maybe
they aren't lying, maybe they believe what they say.
I don't know."

TOM (T.J.) BROOKS: RAWLINS, WYO., SEPTEMBER 23

''Sure I'm happy about the baby coming, but I'm not jumping up and down. I know what kind of a world this is.''

MYRA LOYD: LAS VEGAS, NEV., SEPTEMBER 23

"I can still remember the laugh on my mother's face
and me bust'n out the back door after my bath and rolling
in the snow. Now everyday is a struggle just to hang onto
a small piece of who I am. It seems like when I feel
winter coming on I breathe a little easier."

JOHN RUSSELL: SALT WELLS, NEV., SEPTEMBER 24

"It don't have to be no more than a rock outcrop with
scrub and sagebrush up on the side of a butte. The rock
all busted up and intricate with fissures and frost cracks
and streaks of pyrite and paintbrush and loco weed growing
in the sandy places. It's affection that makes the
difference."

ANNA MAE DOWNS: YARNELL, ARIZ., SEPTEMBER 24

"Folks say this or that, one thing and another. Well, talk's all right. Me, I put my back to the wind. Always have."

R.C. HAMMOND: BIG PINEY, WYO., SEPTEMBER 25

"Work comes first. Even before wife and daughters. Don't seem like there is no other way but work."

JOHN HARPER: RUBY VALLEY, NEV., SEPTEMBER 30

"Seems like most times I got more strength than I can ever use. Like life don't ask me to be strong no more. I just can't understand that."

IRENE DUTT: COALVILLE, UTAH, OCTOBER 3

"It is hurtful. Sometimes down right mean and ugly. But
there's times of an evening when the smell of sage is
coming onto the porch and you can see the lights of town
just a glow beyond the hill and everything is still, so
still you think you can hear the cottonwoods growing down
by the creek. You can't ever be truely happy and you
don't expect to. You find the still moments and hang
onto 'em."

EUGENE DRISCOLL: TONOPAH, NEV., OCTOBER 3

"Each night when I go to bed I say a prayer. I ask the Lord to let me live one more day. I got a lot to do and I want to get it done."

CLARA SWENSON: TEN SLEEP, WYO., OCTOBER 3

"Maybe things would have been different if I had been different. But I'm who I am. I made a lat of mistakes, maybe too many. I don't know. I just wish sometimes I could have seen farther, could have seen things coming and been more ready."

DERN WILLIAMS: TEXAS CITY, TEXAS, OCTOBER 3

"I got a house and a car, I even got a boat. Ain't
none of it worth it. Hell, I hate going to work. You're
nothing on the line, man. Hell, you're less than nothing.
They ain't going to move me up. So that's it. That's all
there is. I'm going to be doing the same crap 'till the
day I die."

IDA WANAMAKER: GALLUP, N.M., OCTOBER 4

"I don't tell people what I do, most times I don't
even tell 'em what I know. This is a country where
people feel damn sure of themselves and damn sure of
their rightness, but they don't know, not really, and
they don't see clear. They're blind to their own selves.
You can't talk to people for five minutes you don't run
up against their ignorance. So I keep to myself, keep
it down inside."

SAM WANAMAKER: GALLUP, N.M., OCTOBER 4

"The white man has a law for everything. He's all the time changing the law, shaping it to his own pleasure.
It's cowardice, plain and simple."

CLAYTON (WACO) WILLIAMS: BONDURANT, WYO., OCTOBER 5

"I been afraid of one thing or another most all my life."

GLADIS (RUBY) COOPER: OAKLAND, CALIF., OCTOBER 5

"I'm glad my boy is dead. I wouldn't want him to raise
his family up in this world. I think the Lord has turned
his back on it. I think He knows it's gone bad and nothing
can't be done to fix it and He's gonna start again fresh
somewheres else."

ARTHUR PRESCOTT: NEEDLES, CA., OCTOBER 6

"There's a lesser devil. Most folks don't know about him but I seen what he can do. He can turn a man bad, turn him mean and strip him. You can fight him but you won't never be the same. He's small and most always invisible but sometimes cats know when he's around."

WILLIAM (DOC) JAMESON: LOS ALAMOS, N.M., OCTOBER 7

"Im not sure of anything anymore. Used to be I thought
I knew a lot. Not now. Now I never get tired of looking
at the sky and wondering at it. What it comes to in the
end is hills, blue sky and clouds."

GEORGIA CUNNINGHAM: MEDICINE BOW, WYO., OCTOBER 7

"It begins right here. Right here in the house with me
and John and the baby. We don't make it right here, it
won't be right anywhere."

LUCAS COE: SWAN VALLEY, IDAHO, OCTOBER 8

"It'll happen in the fall one cold morning. There'll
be frost on the grass and steam rising from the buckrail
fence where sunlight is hitting it. The sky'll be clear
and the mountains sticking up sharp and clean. I'll
feel so god damned wonderful inside and at the same time
all hollow and empty feeling and I'll just start
drinking."

BESSIE CONALLY: PINEDALE, WYO., OCTOBER 8

"It's harder all the time. There's no room left for
dreaming. All the fine good times is gone. There's
things over which a body just don't seem to have much
say. Things happen in this life, things no one could
of seen coming. But there don't seem to be no other
way but to stick with it to the end."

B.J. RAY: MEXICAN HAT, UTAH, OCTOBER 9

"Sometimes when things get so I don't think I'm gonna be
able to stand it, I think of myself running. It's morning
and I'm naked and the air is cool and clear and I'm running
into the sun coming up. I run and run and run and I don't
never look back."

ALVIE BISHOP: BISBEE, ARIZ., OCTOBER 11

"Don't let nobody ever tell you what to do. We all got
the same blood. The Lord made us all. Don't let
nobody put their words in your mouth. If'n the Lord
wanted us all saying the same thing he would a put a
radio in there 'stead of a tongue. If you got a secret,
you keep it. It ain't nobody's business 'ceptin yours
and the Lord's."

JAMES McGREGOR: CODY, WYO., OCTOBER 11

"I open up the garage about seven, break for lunch around
two and walk over to the cafe. I talk with folks there for
a bit and then it's back to work until nine. Then clean up
and home for dinner. I've been a lot of places and done a
lot of things. I don't ever talk about it. There isn't any
need."

EUSTAS CRAYMER: WAMSUTTER, WYO., OCTOBER 12

"Maybe it's 'cause I'm old. I don't know that's just
a guess. I dream all the time now. Strong dreams like
someone's trying to tell me something. I'm afraid to tell
people, afraid of what they might think. Even my wife
don't know."

MAVIS DURETTE: TRES PIEDRAS, N.M., OCTOBER 12

"People don't like sickness and they're afraid of it but
I think we're all born of a kind of sickness we can't
ever get well from. Whatever we are, that sickness is
a part of it, and if we ever do get well we're as good as
dead."

ABBEY MAY LUMEN: WARM SPRINGS, NEV., OCTOBER 13

"Bitterroot, Sweetwater, Two Wells, we pulled that
trailer up one road and down another. Always thinking
that it wasn't always gonna have to be that way, always
thinking it was just between times and things was gonna
change and we wouldn't all the time be eating off picnic
tables and cleaning dishes under pump water. You can
think a thing sometimes, think a thing as hard as you
can, a thing you want, and it gets to where you can't
see for the thinking, can't see what you have until it's
too late. The thing you wanted never come and the thing
you had, whatever it was, is gone off behind you down
the road somewheres and there's no knowing of it
anymore."

CLARA DEBOW HUTCHINS: WHEELER, KAN., OCTOBER 16

"Jim always said I had two left feet but you can't
help it what way you're born and I surely did love to
dance. Any old excuse would do and I'd be into my
party dress and gone. I dragged that poor man to more
going's on than he'd care to remember. But it always
seemed to me that I really was a fine dancer, even if
I knew it weren't the truth."

LEROY DUMONT: BURFORD, WYO.,
OCTOBER 17

"I had this dream one time when I was a boy. There was
this Indian in it. He was young and strong looking and
he come riding up on a big black with his war bonnet
blowing in the wind. He reined that horse in right
where I stood, jumped down and slapped the horse on the
withers. The horse run off in one direction and he
walked away in the other. I never sat down and thought
about it straight, never said to myself in plain english
I was gonna do it, but I know that ever since then I
always tried to walk the way that Indian walked, always
tried to carry myself the way he carried hisself."

MISS. JESSIE BEULARE: WILLS POINT, TEXAS, OCTOBER 18

"Mens loves to talk. They loves to tell high flying
tales 'bout theyselves. You listen to a man, listen
close to what he tells you 'bout what he thinks he
done, 'bout the way he thinks it was, and you be
knowing more 'bout what that man's made up out of
than if'n you'd a been there youself in the flesh
and seen the real truth of it."

JIMMY C. DOBBS: GABBS, NEV.,
OCTOBER 20

"I can see it clear as if it were yesterday. I was camped
by Ninemile Peak, the sheep were settled and I'd eaten dinner
and cleaned up and I was sitting by the fire smoking and
looking up at the stars before turning in. I heard something
coming through the sagebrush on a dead run. I could hear it
breathing heavy and it run right through camp and, just past
the firelight, it turned and screamed. It screamed a high
piercing kind'a scream like a rabbit makes before it dies.
Then everything got quiet. Next morning, soon's it was
light, I was up. Didn't find a thing. No tracks, no blood,
nothing."

WISTIN (DUD) BLACKNER: GRANGER, WYO., OCTOBER 21

''George was hunting sage chicken and got in the car with the gun loaded. Doctors couldn't save my hand or didn't try. I was too young to know which. It was George's gun and he was older but everyone always acted like it was me, like I was born this way.''

LOUELLEN BLACKNER: GRANGER, WYO., OCTOBER 21

"It weren't no one's fault really. Dud was always
like that, he was a sulky kind of child, kind of dark
and never happy and you couldn't figure out why.
George knowed it weren't his fault, it were just one
of those things that happen and I said so. I've always
said and I'll say it now, it was waiting there for Dud,
waiting for him to come to because of the kind of
sulky down in the mouth child he was and if anyone's
to blame for it, well then, I guess he is."

SAM GAMMONS: ECHO, UTAH, OCTOBER 22

"When I was a boy, I had this dog named Dixie. It
was a good dog but it wasn't real bright and it got
hit by a train. How a dog gets itself hit by a train
I'll be damned if I know. When something like that
happened, my mother used to sit me down and say
'Sammy, I know this is hard on you but everything is for
the best in this the best of all possible worlds and
you ought to remember that.' I always thought she meant
it was the best of all possible worlds but I couldn't
see how it was if your dog just got hisself smacked
by a train and killed. Seemed to me it would a been
a darn sight better if your dog was still alive. Now
I think what she was trying to tell me was that it
didn't matter a lick what I thought might' a been
better or might' a been worse, this here world and
what happened in it was all I was gonna get."

MAVIS THORP: BEAUMONT, TEXAS, OCTOBER 23

"I always believed I was headed toward some great
something. That something was going to happen, something
truely wonderful. I never could see what it was. It
wasn't running away to Hollywood or winning a million
dollars or anything like that. It was a feeling I had
of something and it was going to be something truely
everlastingly wonderful. And through all the marriages
and the children I kept watching for it and waiting for
it and always expecting it anyday to be coming up the
front porch steps and knocking on the door. But it
never come."

DAVID (LUKE) RAWLY: HERMOSA BEACH, CALIF., OCTOBER 24

"When I was a boy, my father used to tell me stories about
his father when his father was a boy. There was one that I
always liked about how his father was sent off one time in
the fall to help with the pig butchering at a neighboring
ranch. By the time the butchering was done and the meat
all hanging in the smokehouse, it was two days past when he
was due home. The rancher tied two gunny sacks full of pigs
feet across my grandfather's saddle and told him to git on home
fast because the family would be worried. It was a long way
by the road so he cut up over the mountains and by the time
he was coming down the other side it was dark. Pretty soon
a pack of wolves picked up the scent of those pigs feet and
come after him. Well, he was a good rider and he had a good
horse under him but the wolves kept gaining. So he opened
up one of the gunny sacks with his knife and started throwing
out pigs feet. He rode that way all night, throwing pigs
feet down behind him to slow the wolves. Come sun up
we was a few miles from home, out of pigs feet, his horse
near dead and the wolves on his heels. They kept a pack of
big dogs penned up by the ranch house door and when his
father heard the wolves, he turned those dogs loose.
You can't tell stories like that anymore. You iust can't."

DEWEY WEAVER: COOK CITY, MONT., OCTOBER 25

"Most times I just live with it, but sometimes when
things ain't going right I get so damned mad I could
kick hell. It just comes on me like to make me
crazy. It ain't what happens, it's what's underneath
that, underneath what happens and's supposed to make
things work out. There's supposed to be something,
something that ain't dependent on the weather or how
much money you got in the bank. But there's times when
I can see through things and then there don't appear
to be anything there at all. It's when I think I been
fooling myself and it's just empty underneath everything,
that I get mad enough to kick hell. If it's night and
winter I go onto the back porch and stand there in the
cold and watch the snow coming down. I stand there
until I feel the cold and the dark all through me
down into my bones. Then it's all right. Whether
it's empty under everything or no, it's all right."

GLADIS WHIPPLE: PROVO, UTAH, OCTOBER 25

"Love is all right and that's fine and I'm content
enough but what I really want is to be respected and
paid attention to and to be listened to and accepted
for who I am. It seems a simple enough thing to ask
but it's hard come by."

JOE WATERS: SANDER, ARIZ., OCTOBER 25

"Folks come blowing through here at a pretty good
clip. Hello 'n goodbye. They always in a hurry.
They was too long where they been and they behind
getting to where they going. Trouble with most
folks is they actually believe what they think. I
don't take none of it too serious."

ELROY GRANGER: SPEARFISH, SOUTH DAKOTA, OCTOBER 28

"There's a lot of real evil in this world. Sometimes
it just come on a man. Even if he loves his wife and
children and been regular to church it just come on a
man. You can most always hear it coming. It's like
the rustle of cottonwoods before a storm, a high,
telling kind of sound. A man's got to take hisself
off somewheres then, he's got to get hisself alone
and wrestle with it. If a man's lucky, he'll take
some hard blows and maybe even a bad thumping, but
if he gives as good as he takes and don't hold back,
it'll pass him by."

DEE DEE MAY JUPES: SULPHER BLUFF, TEXAS, OCTOBER 28

"Sometimes I get this voice I can't stop from listening
to. I know when it's coming 'cause I feel restless all
night like I got gas and I don't sleep none too good.
When I get up, first thing I go into the garden and
start to weed'n. I ask it real polite what it want
this time and I listen real polite and time to time
I'll nod my head and 'hmmmmm' it a little. 'You think
so,' I'll say. 'That a fact?' It go on and on but I
keep weed'n and don't let it move me. When it start
in to get'n nasty and talking down right mean trash,
then I speak up sharp. 'I don't know 'bout that myself,'
I'll say. 'I don't know nothing 'bout that and it ain't
none of my business and I doubt it's any of yours.'
That tend to fix it most times. It don't like sass."

TOM BUD: DANIEL, WYO., OCTOBER 29

"The work ain't never done on this ranch and it's most
always hard and struggling to stay even. There's times
when it slows a bit, and you can see some easy space.
Maybe of a Sunday morning, if I don't have to weld any
busted equipment, I'll put on my hip boots and sling a
shovel across my back and get on the old motorcycle and
ride out along the irrigation ditches. Where water's
getting backed up and flooding, I'll stop and clear the
ditch. It's the kind of thing I did down on hands and
knees as a boy. I'll usually take a cold chicken steak
slapped between bread and stop somewheres and eat it.
I like being out under the wide sky and helping the
water a bit, helping it flow. It gives a man a chance
to think, gives him some peace of mind."

RAY HOBBS: JACKPOT, NEV., OCTOBER 30

"At bottom life is scrub sage and dry washes. It don't give me no joy knowing in the end me and nature gonna come even. But a man can go toward his death like he done his life, with his eyes open and his head up."

REV. SAMUAL FLOWERS: STILLWATER, OKLA., OCTOBER 31

"Of the violence in this world one can only say that
it makes a rabid dog look remarkably restrained. One
feels helpless and can only look on in fear and
trembling and curse his God."

COLE JESSUP: SALT FLATS, TEXAS, NOVEMBER 14

"The soul is a funny thing. It don't got any one shape
nor any particular size. It can make itself big as a
barn or small like a pea. It can be strong one minute
and weak and kind'a sickly the next. Some of 'em likes
light and others is shy and prefers the dark. They oft
times like a frisky horse. You don't never break a
good horse, you let him carry you of his own self."

BUSTER DUPREE: DELCAMBRE, LOUISIANA, NOVEMBER 15

"There's snakes. Up the road the mist comes in sometimes. If I gotta go potty I dig a hole in the ground. Ma don't like that. She wants me to fix the door to the coop. I ain't gonna. I'm gonna go to town. Get me an ice cream. It's what I want."

RUBY WILLETT THOMAS: CHULA VISTA, CALIF., NOVEMBER 16

"Daughter, sister, bad girl, I could have been any one
of them but I never was. One instant is all it takes
and your whole life is changed. The car stopped and I
got in. The strange thing is that none of it was against
my will and I grew up happy. We lived quietly like
husband and wife near Dayton, Ohio until the day he
died."

ELIZABETH (LIZA) WHEELER: PALM SPRINGS, CALIF., NOVEMBER 16

"We were happy and I never wanted for anything. He
bought me whatever I wanted and we traveled all the
time and he was devoted to me. In the end when he was
dying, I'd sit by his bed in the hospital day and night
holding his hand. He had tubes running in and out of
him and he was too weak to even hold up his head and
take a sip of water. I'd hold the glass and bend the
straw to his dry lips. I always let him struggle a
minute or two before I let him drink."

CHARLOTTE ANN DODGE: LA BARGE, WYO., NOVEMBER 16

"He'd come through the kitchen door soaking wet and covered head to foot with mud. 'Watch out for my clean floor,' I'd say. And he'd just laugh and grab me around the waist. 'Mamma, where are my pretties?' he'd say. 'Where are my sweet, sweet lovelies?.' And right there he'd unbutton my dress so my breasts filled his big hands. He liked me to hike up my skirt and show my backside going out the door. 'Oh, John,' I'd say but I'd do it and my face would turn beet red. He'd slap his hand down on the table so the dishes rattled and laugh and laugh."

BEN CROWLY: RED LODGE, MONT., DECEMBER 25

"Last thing I remember I was up in the mountains cutting
timber. All of a sudden I went down in the snow like I'd
been kicked in the head. When I come to, I was way
up in the corner of this room on the ceiling looking down.
There were bright lights and I could see my body laying on
a steel table, my chest cut wide open. The doctor was
yelling at the nurse because my heart had stopped or something.
I wasn't afraid, didn't feel any kind of fear at all. Looking
down on myself laying there real peaceful asleep kind'a and
the doctor madder'n hell and the nurses frantic looking, I
had a kind'a pity for 'em all. I didn't have to come back,
didn't necessarily want to, but I did."

www.ingramcontent.com/pod-product-compliance
Lightning Source LLC
Chambersburg PA
CBHW070354200726

48294CB00003B/906